This book belongs to

The accompanying musical audiobook is available for download at

www.montythemaestro.com

For my Parents and Robert -

Thank you for everything. - Gabrielle Amelia Ridgeon

Kate Slater works in mixed media collage

First published in 2015 by GAR Publications
This edition published in 2015 by GAR Publications in association with Albury Books
Albury Court, Albury, Thame, OX9 2LP, United Kingdom
British Library Cataloguing in Publication Data available

ISBN 978-1-910571-37-8

Printed in China

MONTY

the Maestro

and his

~~Marvellous~~

MAGICAL

Orchestra

GABRIELLE
AMELIA RIDGEON   KATE SLATER

In a small dusty workshop on a dark cobbled street
There's a little old man who is earning his keep.
His friends call him Monty and he lives all alone,
Above his own workshop is where he calls home.

His glasses are bent and his hair has turned white
From working all day and all through the night.

He repairs broken instruments and musical toys
But he can't seem to get them to make any noise!

One sunny day Monty woke from his sleep
Feeling better than ever and sprang to his feet!

Monty slid down the drainpipe
to his workshop front door,

And landed to find
a surprise on the floor!

Holding an envelope addressed to "Monty",
He hopped and he cried,
"It's a letter for me!"

In a hurry to open the letter he tore the paper
and squealed with delight when he saw...

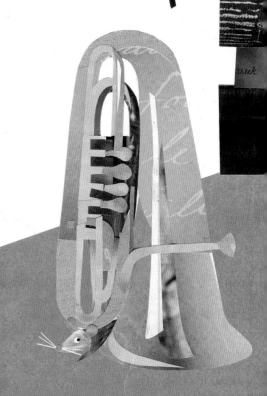

An odd looking stick to wave in the air
And a miniature book on the 'Art of Repair'.

Monty opened the book and turned over each page
To find all of the instruments that play on the stage.

The miniature book then went on to inform that
"The stick was the key if he was to perform

The miraculous job of making them play
All at once as an orchestra day after day."

"Just like the instruments, sticks too have a name.
It will answer to baton", the first page explained.
"It will do what their marvellous maestro believes"
And with that he was ready and rolled back his sleeves.

Monty picked up his baton, worked on his grip,
Waved his hands in the air with his eye on the tip.

"Now listen up Monty, to conduct in time
With a musical beat you must follow my rhyme.

There's a magical secret
for counting in four,
So imagine you're drawing
a line to the floor,

Now sweep to your left
just before you arrive,

Then across to your right...   and curve up to the sky!

"Very good Monty, you must be aware
You're a natural conductor with oodles of flare!
You don't have an orchestra, which isn't much fun
So we'll find you a troop and won't stop 'til we're done.

Your adventure will start if you follow my lead
In reciting this rhyme. Please repeat after me...

I'm Monty the Maestro,
I will show you the way,
To a magical orchestra,
That will blow you away!"

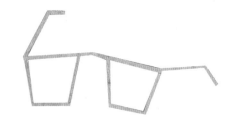

Keep your eyes peeled

Vanessa the Violin

Violet the Viola

Chip the Cello

Digby the Double Bass

For more from Monty and his friends visit

www.montythemaestro.com